The AMAZING DAYS of ABBY HAYES.

The More, the Merrier

Read all the books about me!

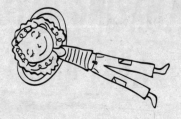

The
AMAZING DAYS
of ABBY HAYES®

The More, the Merrier

ANNE MAZER

AN
APPLE
PAPERBACK

SCHOLASTIC INC.
New York Toronto London Auckland Sydney
Mexico City New Delhi Hong Kong Buenos Aires

To Miko

No part of this publication may be reproduced in whole or in part, or stored in a retrieval system, or transmitted in any form or by any means, electronic, mechanical, photocopying, recording, or otherwise, without written permission of the publisher. For information regarding permission, write to Scholastic Inc., Attention: Permissions Department, 557 Broadway, New York, NY 10012.

ISBN 0-439-35367-X

12 11 10 9   8 9 10/0

Printed in the U.S.A.   40

First Scholastic printing, August 2002

Chapter 1

<u>Reasons my heart wants to have a "Hooray! It's Summer!" party for the entire fifth grade</u>:

1. It'll be fun.

2. All my friends will come.

3. We can celebrate the end of school.

4. We can eat watermelon, ice cream, hamburgers, hot dogs (or tofu dogs for Bethany), and potato salad.

5. The girls can compete against the boys (ha-ha-ha).

6. We can build a bonfire and make s'mores!

* * *

There is only one possible problem: Mom and Dad. Will they understand my reasons for having a party? Will they "listen to my heart"? (Ugh! That sounds like a medical checkup!)

Maybe they'll listen to my lungs or brain or kidneys. They'll all say the same thing. Every part of me wants to throw a party!!!!

What will Mom and Dad say? Will they let me have it? Isabel and Eva throw parties all the time. They are always popular!

I hope Mom and Dad will say yes!

"Guess what?" Abby whispered to her best friends, Jessica and Natalie, in class. Their teacher, Ms. Kantor, was collecting math homework. The three girls had just handed theirs in.

Natalie glanced up from the book she was reading under her desk. "What?"

"I'm going to ask my parents if they'll let me have an end-of-the-year party!" Abby announced.

"You think they'll say yes?" Jessica asked. She pushed a strand of long brown hair away from her face.

"Why not?" Abby said. "My older sisters have parties all the time."

"Lucky," Natalie said, shutting her book and slipping it into her desk. "My parents won't let me or my brother have parties."

"I have all my arguments prepared," Abby said. It helped having a mother who was a lawyer and an older sister who was a debating champ. In ten years of living with them, she had learned a thing or two.

"I hope they agree," Natalie said.

"I'm going to invite the entire fifth grade," Abby continued. "Ms. Kantor's class *and* Ms. McMillan's."

"Everyone?" Jessica asked with a frown. "Even Brianna?"

"It wouldn't be everyone without her," Abby said.

"Ugh," Jessica said.

The three girls glanced over to where Brianna sat, surrounded by a group of admirers. She wore a pale blue lace T-shirt over a short shiny silver skirt. She had on tiny earrings and colored lip gloss.

"My dance recital last night was the *best*," Brianna bragged loudly enough to be heard across the room. "Fifty-two people came to see me."

"I wonder if fifty-two people watched her eat breakfast," Natalie murmured. "She probably chews the best, too."

"If Brianna comes to your party, so will Victoria," Jessica warned Abby. "She's even worse."

"If that's possible," Natalie added.

Victoria was in Ms. McMillan's fifth-grade class. She and Brianna had become friends when they worked on a science fair project together. If Brianna was the best, Victoria was the coolest. She was also the meanest.

Abby shook her head. "No one will be left out," she insisted.

"They'll ruin the party," Jessica predicted.

"No, they won't!" Abby replied. "It'll be such a big crowd, no one will notice them."

"Ha," Natalie said.

Abby scowled at her friends. "If I don't invite them, they'll ruin my life!"

"You have a point," Jessica admitted.

"I wouldn't want Brianna mad at me," Natalie agreed.

Jessica bent over her notebook, then held it up for Abby and Natalie to see. She had doodled a picture of Brianna with a thick, scowling brow and a thundercloud over her head.

"Put a bolt of lightning in her hand," Abby advised Jessica.

Jessica smiled and picked up her pencil again. The three girls crowded around the drawing.

Ms. Kantor clapped her hands. "Back to your seats, everyone!"

Abby looked up. Ms. Bunder, her favorite teacher, had just come into the classroom.

Ms. Bunder came to Ms. Kantor's class once a week, to teach creative writing. She wore black slim-fitting pants and a silk tank top. Her necklace was silver and so were her earrings. Her eyes sparkled as she walked up to the blackboard and began to tape pictures on it.

"What are we doing today?" Mason demanded. He stuck a fat finger into his nose.

"*Eeeeeuuuuu*," Bethany squealed. "Yuk."

Jessica rolled her eyes. "He's *so* disgusting."

Ms. Kantor took a stack of papers and sat down at the back of the room. "Sssshhh!" she said to the class. "Quiet!"

Ms. Bunder taped the last picture to the blackboard and turned to face the fifth-graders. "We're going to write about our rooms," she announced.

"Yay!" Abby cheered. Ms. Bunder could ask her to write about the basement or the attic or the backyard shed. Abby loved writing about *anything*.

Ms. Bunder continued. "I want you to think about your room. What does it look like? Is it a special place? What do you do in your room? How do you feel when you're there?"

"Read!" Natalie said.

"Play cards and watch my hamster," Bethany said.

"Sleep," Tyler said.

"Write in my journal!" Abby cried.

"Is your room the way you want it?" Ms. Bunder asked. "How would you make it different? What kind of room would you like to have when you grow up?"

Brianna raised her hand. "I plan to live in a mansion. It'll have an indoor swimming pool and a movie room and . . ."

Mason burped loudly. "My room will be full of junk," he said.

"His mind already is," Abby murmured.

"Look at the rooms that I just taped on the

board," Ms. Bunder advised. "Maybe they'll inspire you to think about *your* room in a new way."

Abby studied the blackboard. "I don't like those girlie-girl rooms," she whispered to Natalie, pointing to a picture of a bedroom done up in pink, with a canopy bed and frilly curtains.

"Me, neither," Natalie whispered back. "I'd like to live in a chemistry lab. Or a castle."

Abby stared at a picture of a room painted in black-and-white zebra stripes. "Isn't that one great?"

"I hate it!" Jessica said. "It'd make me dizzy to live there."

"I'd want to draw in all the white spaces," Natalie said. "Or splash paint on them." She peered down at her white sneakers, which were covered with splotches of color. "Just like my sneakers."

"Okay, let's get started," Ms. Bunder said. "This is an assignment that you might like to complete at home. It's due next week."

"It's *home*work," Abby joked. "Get it?"

Her friends rolled their eyes.

"Casey would get it," Abby said.

"I thought you didn't like him," Natalie said.

Abby shrugged. "He's okay."

Casey was in the other fifth-grade class. He and

Abby had been science fair partners. At first they hadn't gotten along, but Abby had come to like him. He had the same sense of humor that she had.

"Are you inviting him to your party?" Jessica asked.

"Of course!" Abby exclaimed. "And Sarah, too."

Sarah had been Jessica's science fair partner. She and Jessica had become friends while working on a project about the stars and pollution.

"Good," Jessica said. For the first time since they had started talking about the party, she smiled at Abby.

Ms. Bunder walked over to Abby's desk. "Are you thinking about your room?" she asked.

"I'm thinking about my Hooray! It's Summer! party," Abby replied. "Maybe I'll have it in my room. Or maybe not." Forty or fifty kids wouldn't fit in her room. At least, not all at once.

"It sounds like fun," Ms. Bunder said with a smile. "Now start working on the assignment."

Abby picked up her purple pen and began to write down her thoughts about her room.

What were they, anyway?

My room: It has two windows, a door, and a closet. (Exciting.)

My room: It has a floor covered with a rug. There's a bedspread on the bed and curtains on the windows. (Wow.)

My room: I go to sleep there. (Snore.)

This is the most boring essay I have ever written, and I think I am going to stop writing now before I put myself to slee—

Abby dropped her pen with a clatter. Just a minute ago, she had been excited about this new assignment from Ms. Bunder. But now she didn't know what to write.

Wasn't her room special? Why wasn't there anything to say about it?

Chapter 2

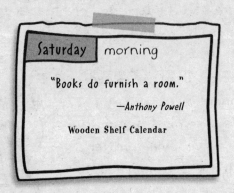

Saturday | morning

"Books do furnish a room."
—Anthony Powell

Wooden Shelf Calendar

So do calendars! In my room, I have only one bookcase, but walls of calendars.

<u>What I see when I look at my room</u>:
1. Calendars
2. Calendars
3. More calendars
4. And . . . you get the idea!

If I write about my room for Ms. Bunder's creative writing assignment, OF COURSE I have to write about my calendars! Why didn't I think of that in the *first place? Because I have been thinking about my party!*

Casey Hoffman dribbled the basketball down the Hayes driveway, passed it to Abby, and cheered as she made a basket.

"Your shots are getting better, Hayes," he said.

"Follow-through helps, Hoffman," Abby told him.

Casey nodded. He had dark hair, dark eyes, and ears that stuck out just a bit. Half an hour ago, he had rung Abby's doorbell and asked her to play basketball.

"Too bad Alex isn't here," Abby said. "He'll be mad that he missed you."

"Tell him we're playing baseball tonight in the park. He can join us." Casey tossed the ball through the hoop.

"Sure," Abby said, retrieving the ball. "He'll like that."

Abby's younger brother worshiped Casey. He followed him around and hung on his every word. As far as Abby was concerned, Casey was just *okay*; she liked him some of the time.

All right, she liked him *most* of the time. He wasn't annoying like Mason and Tyler and Zach. He wasn't giggly and hamster-crazy like Bethany. He wasn't better than she was at everything like her SuperSibs. He got most of her jokes. Even when her friends didn't think she was funny, Casey did.

"Did I tell you about my party?" she asked.

"Is it your birthday?" Casey frowned. "I'm not very good at figuring out presents."

"I want to have a Hooray! It's Summer! party," Abby explained. "I want to invite the entire fifth grade. We'll have it in my backyard. If my parents let me," she added.

"Great!" Casey said. "I hope they do." He threw the ball to Abby.

"Me, too," Abby said. "I'm asking them tonight." She took a deep breath. Her parents *had* to say yes.

"What are you planning?" Casey asked. "Movies? Volleyball? Charades?"

"We'll build a bonfire and make s'mores," Abby said. "We'll play games and talk."

"That sounds like fun," Casey began, when an all too familiar voice interrupted him.

"Abby and Casey. Together at last," Victoria cooed.

Victoria and Brianna stood at the edge of the driveway. The two best-dressed girls in the fifth grade both wore flowered capri pants, lace-edged T-shirts, colored bangles, and shiny lip gloss.

"They're a matching set," Abby said under her breath. Casey began to laugh.

"Casey and Abby," Brianna sighed. "The two of you just can't stay apart."

"The two of us just have to shoot hoops," Abby retorted. She tossed the ball back to Casey, who threw it into the basket.

"Hoops? You're, like, totally on a date," Victoria said.

"We're on a fig," Abby said.

"Dried or fresh?" Casey asked.

"*What* are they talking about?" Victoria asked Brianna.

Brianna shrugged. "Who knows?"

Victoria turned to Abby. "I, like, heard about your party."

"I haven't gotten permission yet," Abby warned.

"My parents let me have all the parties I want," Brianna boasted. "We have them catered."

"Is this an exclusive party?" Victoria asked. "Are you inviting only the coolest kids?"

"I'm inviting the entire fifth grade. It's a Hooray! It's Summer! party," Abby explained.

"You're inviting everyone?" Victoria asked. "Like, boys?"

Abby nodded her head.

"*Fifth*-grade boys?"

"Yes," Abby said. "Mason, Tyler, Zach, Jonathan, Casey . . ."

"Why don't you invite sixth-grade boys?" Victoria suggested. "They're, like, totally better."

"I invite sixth- and seventh-grade boys to *my* parties," Brianna bragged. "Are you having dancing? Or a band?"

"We're having games and a picnic," Abby said.

"Games?" Brianna said. "What kind?"

"Volleyball and races and kickball . . ."

Victoria wrinkled her nose. "That's so, like, elementary school."

"Hayes will throw a great party." Casey leaped to her defense. "Everyone will have a good time."

"Thanks, Hoffman," Abby said.

"Hayes? Hoffman?" Brianna repeated. "Are you two for real?"

"They're, like, *so* adorable," Victoria sneered.

"Will you both come to my party?" Abby asked, trying to change the subject. "I mean, if my parents say yes."

She hoped Brianna and Victoria would say no.

"Like, you know, if I'm not *totally* busy," Victoria said.

"Without us, your party won't be the same," Brianna added.

"It sure won't," Abby agreed.

Victoria checked her watch. "Brianna!" she squealed. "We have to get back to my house. My cousin is going to be there in, like, fifteen minutes."

Brianna sighed. "And leave Abby alone with her boyfriend?"

"He's *not* my boyfriend," Abby insisted.

"Sure, he isn't," Brianna smirked.

"Good-bye, lovebirds," Victoria said. "Come *on*, Brianna!" She grabbed Brianna by the arm and pulled her onto the sidewalk.

"Tweet, tweet!" Abby called.

As they disappeared down the street, Abby turned to Casey. "They're, like, *so* obnoxious!"

"Yep," Casey agreed. He picked up the basketball and tossed it to her.

Abby threw it hard. It bounced off the backboard. She threw the ball again and missed entirely.

"They're going to ruin my party if they come," she

said, frowning. "Jessica already said so. She's probably right."

"Maybe they won't even show up."

Abby brightened. "Really?"

"Your party is so, like, elementary school," Casey mimicked. "It's, like, totally for babies."

Abby passed him the ball. "I'll have a kindergarten party. We'll take naps, build blocks, and play Farmer in the Dell."

"That'll keep them away, Hayes." Casey swished the ball into the basket.

"And everyone else, too."

Casey grinned. "I don't think so. I bet lots of kids in my class will come."

"What can I do about Brianna and Victoria?" Abby asked.

"Don't worry about them," Casey said.

"Right," Abby agreed. She took the ball and shot it into the basket.

It *was* her party, not Brianna's or Victoria's! And it was going to be a great party! If her parents let her have it.

"When are you going to get permission?" Casey asked.

"Soon," Abby promised.

Chapter 3

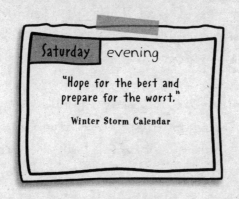

Saturday | evening

"Hope for the best and
prepare for the worst."

Winter Storm Calendar

No! I will <u>only</u> hope for the best: a
party (DUH!) with everyone there. I will
<u>not</u> prepare for the worst: my parents' re-
fusal.

I won't even think about it. They
<u>CAN'T</u> say no! I'd rather have ten Bri-
annas and thirty Victorias attend my party
than have no party at all!

<u>The Great Party Debate</u>
Taking place in the Hayes living room.
Now! In living color!

* * *

The contestants:

1. Paul Hayes and Olivia Hayes, the parents of four children

2. Abby Hayes, the middle child

The odds are stacked against Abby Hayes. She must take on two adults—and one of them is a lawyer! But the brave ten-year-old will not let it stop her from arguing why she deserves to throw a party for the entire fifth grade.

The three contestants sit down together. Paul Hayes sips his coffee. Olivia Hayes squirts lotion on her palm and rubs it into her hands. Abby Hayes pulls at a hangnail.

After a few exciting moments like this, Abby boldly strikes the first blow.

"I want to throw a party for the entire fifth grade," she declares.

"_NO!_" the Hayes parents exclaim simultaneously.

Will the debate end right here? Will Abby run to her room in tears?

No. She is prepared! She has anticipated her parents' reaction and has worked out her arguments in advance.

Abby recites a list of the parties her twin ninth-grade SuperSisters have thrown in the last six months alone.

"Eva gave parties for the lacrosse team, the softball team, and the swim team. Isabel had parties for the debate team, the student council, the drama club, and the honor society."

Olivia Hayes is not impressed. "Those were small parties," she points out. "You want a large party."

"So???" Abby retorts.

This brilliant reply fails to impress her parents.

Abby unveils her next argument.

"Seven parties of approximately twenty people each equals one hundred and forty people, more or less, entertained at our house by my twin sisters." Abby rattles off the statistics. "That equals a SuperSib Super Bash three point five times bigger than the party I'm asking for!"

"Your math is improving," Paul Hayes comments. "However, seven small- to medium-sized parties can't be exchanged for one big one."

"Why <u>not</u>?" Abby demands.

"<u>Because,</u>" her parents reply.

Stunned by her parents' logic, Abby says nothing. For a moment, the debate appears to be at a standstill, with the Hayes parents winning.

Suddenly, in a surprise recovery, Abby jumps to her feet and marches up and down the living room.

"Fifth-graders have a right to parties as much as ninth-graders! Especially when there are two of them and only one of me!

"Eva and Isabel had seven separate parties this year! I had zero! Do you think this is fair? Or just? Or right?" she asks.

The Hayes parents sigh.

Olivia Hayes appeals to her middle daughter. "Are you sure you don't want a small party? Why don't you invite Jessica, Natalie, and Bethany for a sleepover?"

Abby Hayes holds firm. "I want a big party or nothing."

Paul Hayes frowns. Olivia Hayes appears to be thinking. (Or perhaps she's worrying about a court appearance tomorrow?) Abby Hayes crosses her fingers and recites all the magic words she knows.

Olivia Hayes speaks first. "I'd like to say no, but your arguments are irrefutable."

"Huh?" Abby says.

"That means no one can disagree with what you've just said," Paul Hayes explains.

"Okay. Sure. Whatever." Abby wonders why her parents are throwing new vocabulary words at her right now.

Her mother smiles.

"Irrefutable," Abby repeats, just in case this is the magic word that will make her parents say yes. "Will you let me have the party?"

Paul Hayes thinks about it. "It'll be a lot of work," he warns her. "Are you up for it?"

"Yes!" Abby cries.

"You'll be responsible for planning and invitations," Olivia Hayes adds. "And you'll have to clean up, too."

"Of course!!!" Abby promises. "I'll do anything to have a party with all my friends. I'll scrub floors, I'll wash windows, I'll even mow the lawn."

Paul and Olivia Hayes exchange glances. Abby holds her breath.

"Yes, you can," they (<u>finally</u>) say.

"Thank you! Thank you! Thank you!" Abby flings her arms around both parents and kisses them. "You're the best parents who ever lived!"

<u>VICTORY!</u>

Hooray! Hooray! <u>Hooray!</u> Was it really that easy? They didn't make me promise to do thirty years of hard labor or even one weekend of sweeping out the garage or basement. (Ha-ha-ha.) All I have to do is plan, send out invitations, and clean up. A piece of cake! Speaking of cake, I better think about what kind I want.

Chocolate? Or vanilla? Or carrot cake? Or orange or lemon cake? And what kind of decorations should it have?

I also have to come up with a menu. And decide on games. And design the invitations.

I have a lot of decisions to make! And the party is only a few weeks away!

Chapter 4

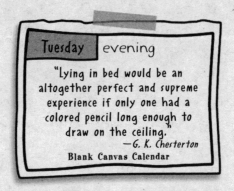

Tuesday evening

"Lying in bed would be an altogether perfect and supreme experience if only one had a colored pencil long enough to draw on the ceiling."
—G. K. Chesterton
Blank Canvas Calendar

I agree! Why don't they sell six-foot pencils in stationery stores??? Or charcoal sticks as big as stilts? Or telescoping paintbrushes?

<u>What I would draw on my ceiling (if I could)</u>:

1. My friends
2. Myself (wearing earrings!)
3. My kitten, T-Jeff
4. Purple swirls

＊　＊　＊

<u>What I wouldn't draw or write on my ceiling</u>:
1. My journal entries
2. My party invitations
3. My essay for creative writing

I have to finish my creative writing essay before I print out party invitations. I wish my parents didn't keep track of my homework!

I have only written one paragraph so far. It's about my calendars (of course). I wonder what my friends are writing about <u>their</u> rooms?

Abby closed her journal and lay back on her bed. For a moment, she stared at the blank ceiling. She imagined it covered with purple swirls, like tinted clouds. She'd love to wake up to a purple, billowy ceiling.

"A purple, billowy ceiling," she said out loud. She reached for the draft of her essay and wrote the words down one side of the paper.

She reread the paragraph she had already written.

In my room, I'm surrounded by time. My calendars are like trees that drop their leaves every thirty days. Every month I have new scenery on my walls.

That was fine — but she had nothing else, except "purple billowy ceiling." Ms. Bunder wouldn't accept it, and neither would her parents!

Abby sat up. She began to write again.

If I didn't have my calendars, my room would be a plain, ordinary room. No one would know anything about me.

No one would know that I have a cat. T-Jeff's food dish and water bowl and kitty litter are in Isabel's room.

No one would know that I love to write. I keep my purple journal hidden where my spying SuperSisters can't find it and read it.

No one would know that I love purple, either! I have only a few purple things:
1. My journal
2. My pen
3. A bear that Grandma Emma gave me

4. Some barrettes and hair clips
5. A small plastic fortune-telling ball
I wish I had a purple billowy ceiling! I wish I had a purple rug and purple curtains! I wish I could turn my room into a Palace of Purple!

Abby put down her pen. She picked up the paper and went to find her parents.

"Abby! Do you know where my tennis racket is?" Eva asked. She was dressed in shorts and a T-shirt. Her hair was pulled back into a ponytail. "I've been looking all over for it!"

"I haven't seen it," Abby said. "Do you know where Mom and Dad are?"

Eva shrugged. "Try the backyard."

Abby ran downstairs. Behind her, Eva yelled for her twin. "*Isabel!* Where's my tennis racket?"

In the backyard, her father was digging a vegetable plot. Her mother was pruning rosebushes.

"I finished my creative writing essay!" Abby announced, waving the draft in her father's direction. He was the one who usually checked her schoolwork. "All my other homework is done. May I print out the party invitations now?"

Paul Hayes put down the shovel. "Let's see what you've written," he said.

"It's the rough draft," Abby explained, handing him the paper. "I'll copy it over tomorrow."

Her father frowned as he read the essay. "It's a little short," he commented. "Especially for you."

"I don't have much to say about my room!" Abby answered. "Unless I quoted from all the calendars. Ms. Bunder would rather have me use my own words."

"She has a point," her father said. He looked at the essay again. "This seems fine."

"Hooray!" Abby cried. "May I use your computer?"

"Did you empty the dishwasher?" her mother called.

"Yes, Mom! I've done *all* my work!"

Her mother nodded. Her father handed back the essay. "I'll set you up on the computer as soon as I wash my hands."

"I can do it, Dad. I know what to do."

"Okay," her father said. "Just remember to exit when you're done."

"I *know*, Dad!" Abby began. She was about to tell him how well she understood the computer and its programs when Eva and Isabel appeared on the back porch.

Eva looked furious. So did Isabel.

"Mom! Dad! Isabel used my tennis racket!" Eva cried. "Without permission!"

"Eva! You said — " Isabel began. Her long dark hair was pulled back with a pink-and-silver barrette. She pulled impatiently on a stray lock as she faced her twin.

"I *didn't*!" Eva insisted.

"You did!" Isabel said. "Why are you bothering Mom and Dad with this?" she added primly. "Can't we work it out on our own?"

"NO!" Eva said.

Olivia Hayes put down her pruning shears. "Don't you have your own tennis racket, Isabel?"

"I did, but — "

"She lent it!" Eva finished her twin's sentence.

"And then Eva said — "

"I said nothing! I never gave you permission to use mine!"

"Not true!" Isabel retorted.

"Is too!" Eva shot back.

Abby glanced at her father. He had picked up his shovel and was breaking up a clod of dirt.

"Thief!" Eva cried.

"Liar!" Isabel accused.

Their mother interrupted. "You can use *my* tennis racket whenever you want, Isabel. Leave your sister's alone. End of argument."

The twins frowned at each other one last time. Then Eva ran back into the house, slamming the door behind her.

Isabel followed, with a second slam of the door.

"Another day, another argument," Paul Hayes said. "When will it end?"

"I'm going on the computer to print out the party invitations," Abby said. She hoped her sisters didn't plan on using it, too. She didn't want to tangle with either of them right now.

"There's rainbow-colored paper in my study," her mother said. "Take as much as you need."

"Great!" Abby said. She ran up the back porch stairs and opened the kitchen door.

Isabel and Eva were sitting at the kitchen table, drinking apple juice and chatting as if nothing had happened.

"Uh, hi," Abby said nervously. Her sisters were like two bombs that might explode at any moment. Or not.

"We're talking about your party, Abby," Eva said.

"You are?"

"How did you get Mom and Dad to agree to it?" Isabel studied her younger sister. "They never let *us* invite the entire fifth grade!"

"We're impressed," Eva continued. "We want to know your technique."

Abby poured herself a glass of juice. "Irrefutable logic," she said.

"*What?*" Eva asked.

"She out-argued them, dummy," Isabel informed her.

"Dummy?" Eva repeated. She glared at her twin.

"Never mind, silly," Isabel said. "What kinds of arguments did you use, Abby?"

Should she tell Isabel and Eva that she used *them* to get permission? Probably not. Abby drank her juice in one gulp and set the empty glass on the counter.

"Mathematical arguments," Abby replied. She took a step toward the kitchen door. "I have to go print out the invitations now."

Upstairs in her father's office, Abby turned on the computer monitor. She opened the program to make greeting cards.

First she flipped through illustrations. Did she want balloons? Or soccer balls? Or flowers? Or cakes? Or trees and ponds? Or teddy bears?

And what kind of type did she want?

Calligraphy? Plain? Gothic? Italic? Script? Block letters?

There were so many decisions to make!

Abby typed out the words "Hooray! It's Summer!" and tried them out in different fonts.

She added illustrations and took them away.

She experimented with textured backgrounds and plain ones.

Using her mother's rainbow paper, she printed out several trial invitations. None of them was quite right.

"Are you *still* here?" Isabel asked.

"I thought you'd be done hours ago," Eva added.

Abby glanced at the clock. Two hours had passed. It seemed like only a few minutes.

"They're almost done," she lied. "Just a few more minutes."

Isabel picked up one of the invitations. "You need help," she said.

Eva peered over her shoulder. "Why don't you make the type smaller and the background brighter?"

"I think the type should be larger," Isabel disagreed.

Abby snatched the invitation from her older sisters. "It's mine," she said. "I'll do it the way I want."

Isabel shrugged. "If that's how you feel."

"The illustrations are crooked," Eva said.

Abby frowned. "I don't want any help."

"Why not?" Isabel asked. "We've got experience and knowledge."

Eva slung her arm around her twin. "Yeah, we've got Twin Power."

"No!" Abby said.

Her sisters didn't listen. They grabbed another invitation from the printer and began to criticize it.

Chapter 5

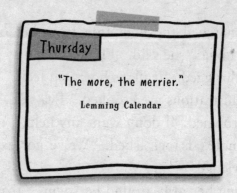

> **Thursday**
>
> "The more, the merrier."
>
> **Lemming Calendar**

The more <u>what</u>, the merrier?

1. The more kids at my party, the merrier.

2. The more calendars on my walls, the merrier.

3. The more sisters helping print out my invitations, the

    . . . gloomier? . . . harder? . . . longer? . . . stupider?

None of these words sums up what happened when Eva and Isabel insisted on improving my invitations.

They argued for half an hour over

whether it should be Hooray! It's Summer!
or Hooray for Summer!

They argued whether I should print
swimming pools in the background or tennis
rackets.

They argued whether I should print all
the invitations on purple paper or rainbow
paper or plain white with colored designs.

They argued. . . .

AAAAAAARRRRRRGGGGGGGHHHHH!

Twin Power?? No, Twin Powder Keg!

If Isabel and Eva hadn't been "helping"
me, I would have finished the invitations
on Tuesday night.

Instead, I had to finish printing them
out on Wednesday night, when my sisters
were out of the house. I hurried through
my homework and quickly copied my creative
writing essay.

(I didn't do as good a job on my writing as usual. I hope Ms. Bunder will understand!)

Now that they're finally done, the invitations look great!!! They are printed on Mom's rainbow-colored paper in a calligraphy font that Isabel suggested. There are balloons and stars in the background.

Eva told me to put the invitations in a plastic bag to protect them. (My sisters <u>did</u> have a few good ideas!)

The invitations are in my backpack, waiting to be passed out at recess, after class with Ms. Bunder. I can't wait!!!!!

In front of the class, Bethany held up a lovingly drawn picture of her hamster, Blondie, in her cage. "My room," she began. "My room is a deluxe hamster suite. My room is Blondie-centered. My room is hamster heaven."

The class listened attentively.

"We're going to take a tour of the rooms of the fifth grade," Ms. Bunder had said at the beginning of class. "We'll visit everyone's room — even if we never visit their house!"

Everyone cheered. Except Abby. She stared down at her desk.

It was one thing to hand in an assignment she'd written in a hurry. It was another to read it out loud. If she had known, she never would have rushed. She would have taken more time. She would have given it more thought. There must have been something else to say about her room.

Bethany concluded her essay with a description of a poster of Brianna hanging from her wall. "Yay, Brianna," Bethany said.

"You forgot to mention that it's a *signed* poster," Brianna corrected her.

As Bethany slid back into her seat, Natalie jumped up. "Can I go next, Ms. Bunder?" she cried.

Ms. Bunder nodded.

Natalie hurried to the front of the class. Her short dark hair was tousled and unruly. She began reading from a wrinkled, folded paper.

"My room is a Harry Potter shrine," she began. "I have Harry Potter sheets, curtains, clock, slippers, and bathrobe. I have read each of the Harry Potter books ninety-two times. I also have an international Harry Potter shelf, with books in seven different languages: Japanese, French, German, Spanish, Danish, Arabic, and Chinese. No, I can't read them, but maybe I will someday.

"Aside from that, I have a table with chemistry equipment and a bookcase filled with mystery and fantasy novels. I have a closet full of capes, swords, gowns, and unusual hats. And a hamster named Madame Curie."

"What an exciting room!" Ms. Bunder said.

The fifth-graders applauded. Abby sighed. Natalie's room sounded so — *Natalie*!

Mason lumbered to the front of the class. "My room is a disaster zone," he began.

The class laughed.

"My room looks like a hurricane hit it. There are clothes piled three feet high on the bed." Mason grinned at the class. "It's decorated with old pizza boxes, a broken lamp shade, and a cracked window. There's a DANGER sign on the door. If you walk in, you may not come out. Enter if you dare!"

"That was a very good description!" Ms. Bunder said. "But I hope you stretched the truth!"

"I stretched it like Silly Putty!" Mason said. He high-fived Zach on the way back to his seat.

"Next?" Ms. Bunder said. "Any volunteers? Brianna?"

"My essay is called 'Beauty and the Best,' " Brianna announced. She paused to flip her hair over her shoulder and to smile professionally at the class.

"My room is a reflection of me. It is the best room I have ever seen. I have my own audiovisual center, a large-screen television, a DVD player, a private phone line, a computer, and a canopy bed decorated with Belgian lace."

"It's 'Beauty and the Boast,' " Natalie whispered to Abby.

"Yes!" Abby agreed.

There was polite applause from the class and a "Yay, Brianna" from Bethany when Brianna finished her essay.

"That's quite a room, Brianna," Ms. Bunder said. She scanned the class. "Who hasn't read their essay?"

Abby squirmed in her seat.

"You're awfully quiet today, Abby," Ms. Bunder said. "Why don't you read next?"

Abby slowly made her way to the front of the room, unfolded her paper, and began to read.

"In my room, I'm surrounded by time. My calendars are like trees that drop their leaves every thirty days. Every month I have new scenery on my walls."

Her face was burning. No one else in the class had written anything like this. Would they laugh at her? Or just not get it?

She rushed through the rest of the essay, concluding, "I wish I could turn my room into a Palace of Purple!"

Abby glanced at her teacher and slunk back to her seat.

"Very interesting, Abby," Ms. Bunder said.

"Interesting," Abby repeated to herself. That was a word that everyone said. It meant nothing. It probably meant less than nothing.

"I liked it," Natalie whispered.

Abby grimaced. Natalie was her friend. Of course she liked it!

No matter what anyone said, Abby knew that her essay was one of the least exciting in the class. Not because she couldn't write — but because there was nothing to write about!

Her room wasn't a Harry Potter shrine, a disaster zone, or a hamster-lover's paradise. It wasn't a tree house — except in her imagination — or a palace of purple. It didn't reflect her personality or her tastes. It didn't have anything to do with Abby Hayes.

Her room was plain and ordinary, with a bunch of calendars stuck on the walls.

Chapter 6

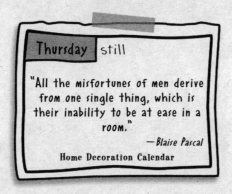

Thursday | still

"All the misfortunes of men derive from one single thing, which is their inability to be at ease in a room."
—*Blaise Pascal*
Home Decoration Calendar

I am <u>not</u> at ease in my room! Especially after hearing my classmates' essays!

Does this mean that I'm going to have a misfortune? (*Noooooo!!!!*)

Does this mean that my party will be a disaster? (Help!!!!!)

Does this mean that my classmates will ask to see my room during the party? (*Noooooo!!!!!* Help!!! That would be a misfortune *AND* a disaster!)

* * *

<u>What My Classmates Will Probably Do</u>
<u>When They See My Room</u>:
1. Laugh
2. Yawn
3. Run for the door

Maybe I should put a "Danger" sign on the door. Or orange police tape.

What I need is a "Danger! Boring Room!" sign.

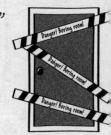

(Good thing I have my party to think about!)

"Party invitations!" Abby called. She stood in the middle of the playground and held up a folded stack of colorful cards. "Come and get them!"

"Where's mine?" Mason demanded. "I'm a party animal!"

"I know that," Abby said, handing him a lime green invitation.

"Cool!" Tyler said, reading over Mason's shoulder. "A party for the whole fifth grade!"

Abby gave him an invitation. "I'm planning it myself."

"Make sure there's plenty of food," Zach advised her.

"Especially if you're inviting boys," Rachel added.

"Girls eat just as much as boys!" Megan protested.

"Yeah!" Mason burped in agreement.

"Eeeuuu! Disgusting!" Rachel said.

One by one, Abby distributed the invitations to her classmates. Then she went to find Jessica.

Jessica was upside down on the rings next to Sarah, who hung by her hands. Jessica swung by her knees. Her long brown hair trailed along the ground.

"Got party invitations?" Abby asked. She waved them in front of the two girls.

Jessica pulled herself up and dropped to the ground. "I can't believe your parents said yes!"

Abby nodded. "I'm planning the whole party by myself. They said I could do anything within reason."

"What about without?" Jessica teased.

"All my plans have a reason!" Abby said. "To have a good time!"

Sarah somersaulted over the rings and landed on her feet. Her face was red and perspiring.

"I hope you can come to my party," Abby said, giving her an invitation. She didn't know Sarah very well. Once or twice they had played soccer together. She was Jessica's friend, not hers.

Sarah pushed back a lock of damp hair from her forehead. She glanced at the invitation and stuffed it in her shorts pocket. Then she jumped back onto the rings and swung back and forth.

"Can you can get all the way across without falling?" Jessica challenged her.

"I can!" Sarah leaped for the next ring.

The two girls seemed to have forgotten about Abby.

"See you," Abby said. She hurried across the playground to look for Bethany and Natalie.

They were deep in conversation next to the slide.

"Hamsters are nocturnal," Bethany was saying. "They sleep during the day and play all night."

"I noticed," Natalie said, yawning.

"Party! Party! Party!" Abby interrupted them.

"Oh, great," Natalie said.

"Fun!" Bethany said. "I can't wait!"

Brianna came up behind them. Abby turned to give her an invitation.

"Colored xerox paper?" Brianna said, wrinkling her nose. "My party invitations are custom-printed on handmade paper with calligraphic lettering."

"I remember those," Bethany said.

"Oh, hello there," Brianna said, acknowledging her best friend with a wave of her hand. *"Comment ça va?"*

"Ssssuh *what*?" Natalie asked.

"It's French," Brianna informed her. *"Je parle le français."*

"Iay eferpray igpay atinlay," Natalie retorted. "I prefer pig latin."

"How about guinea pig latin?" Abby grinned at Bethany.

"Is there such a thing as hamster latin?" Bethany asked hopefully.

Brianna rolled her eyes. "Do you have any other topic of conversation besides hamsters?" she demanded.

"Like, I don't think so," Victoria said nastily as she joined the group of girls.

"Victoria!" Brianna squealed, turning her back on Bethany.

"Brianna!" Victoria squealed back. "I have the coolest new CD to play for you. It's by Tiffany Crystal."

"Oooooh!" Brianna shrieked. "I love her! She's the greatest!"

"The Tiffany Crystal concert is, like, soon," Victoria said. "Are you going?"

"I have free tickets," Brianna announced. "My cousin knows the electrician on Tiffany's tour."

"We're going together," Bethany said. "Aren't we, Brianna?"

Brianna didn't reply. She ignored her best friend. Instead, she linked arms with Victoria. The two girls began to sing one of Tiffany's platinum hits.

"Nasty sugar sweet," they blared.

Bethany looked depressed.

"Have an invitation to my party," Abby said. She thrust one into Victoria's hand.

"Wow, this is, like, so exciting," Victoria said sarcastically. "I can hardly wait."

Abby straightened up. "I'm having live music, a tent, and prizes!" she said. "My party is going to be *great*!"

"Esyay," Natalie agreed in pig latin.

"I'm glad your party isn't on the same day as the Tiffany Crystal concert," Bethany said. "Brianna and I love Tiffany."

Brianna turned to Victoria. "Have you seen my new lip gloss collection?"

"It's the best," Bethany said eagerly. "Brianna has the biggest lip gloss collection in the fifth grade."

"Come on, Brianna, let's go," Victoria said, making a face. "We can't talk here. Hamster ears are listening."

Without saying good-bye, the two girls walked away. Bethany trailed behind them for a few moments, then veered off toward a bench.

Natalie and Abby went over to join her.

"I hate Tiffany Crystal," Natalie said, sitting down next to Bethany. "She can't sing."

"She's okay," Bethany mumbled. "I just hope Brianna doesn't invite Victoria to the concert with us."

"Like, why not?" Abby mimicked. "Victoria is so, like, totally *sweet*!"

Bethany tried to smile.

Abby slung her arm around Bethany's shoulder. "Cheer up, Bethany. You're *so* much nicer than Victoria!"

"Yeah," Natalie agreed.

Bethany frowned. "Do you think Brianna knows that?"

Natalie and Abby looked at each other. They didn't say anything.

Abby got up to give out the rest of the invitations. She found Casey and asked him to hand out some to his classmates. When she returned, Bethany and Natalie were talking about hamsters again.

"Can we talk about another animal for a change?" Abby joked. "Like emus, ocelots, or mongooses?"

"Are you really having live music, a tent, and prizes at your party?" Natalie asked Abby.

"Well — "

"Don't worry, Abby. Your party will be *almost* as good as Brianna's," Bethany reassured her.

"Thanks, Bethany." Abby frowned. "I wish I hadn't promised all those things!"

She scuffed her foot in the dirt. "The live music is going to be a boom box," Abby said slowly. "The tent will be Alex's Cub Scout tent, and the prizes will probably be a bunch of pencils!"

"It still sounds like fun," Natalie said.

Abby just hoped that Brianna and Victoria wouldn't make fun of her party. They had a way of getting lots of kids on their side.

She also hoped that they wouldn't ask to see her room! Or go up there before she knew what they were doing.

She especially hoped that they wouldn't be too mean to Bethany.

Could someone put them in solitary confinement on the day of her party?

Chapter 7

Friday evening

"What is the hardest task in the world? To think!"

—Ralph Waldo Emerson

Impossible Dreams Calendar

7:15 p.m. I am trying to think about my room.

What does my room need? What can I do to make it better? Think! Think! Think!

What is in my room (aside from calendars):

1. A lamp (with peeling, ugly paint)

2. A bureau (with clothes spilling out of its drawers)

3. A bed (not made)

4. A chair (only one leg dented)
5. A mirror (smeared with fingerprints)
6. A clock (six minutes fast)
7. A desk (piled with papers and books)

Is there a 911 Room? My room needs first aid! It needs emergency care! Is there a room doctor in the house?

I want a room that I can show off to my friends and classmates!

I want a room that everyone will talk about!

I want a room that I will love spending time in!

I want an Abby room instead of an Anyone room.

<u>What I'd like in my room (aside from calendars)</u>:
1. A petting zoo
2. A water slide and a roller coaster

3. A basketball court
4. An earring store
5. My own computer
6. A bubble gum machine

Sure. Right. Yeah.

<u>What I could actually do to my room</u>
<u>(aside from buying more calendars)</u>:
1. Make the bed
2. Vacuum the floor
3. Clear off the desk

Uh. Duh. Boring!!!
   If I clean my room now, I'll have to
clean it again before the party. (Why waste
energy? Once is enough!)

<u>Other ideas</u>:

Okay, never mind.

7:42 p.m.

Minutes I have been thinking: 27

Number of useful ideas I have had: 0

Will put self in <u>Hayes Book of World Records</u> for "Fiercest Brain Activity with Fewest Results."

Thinking <u>is</u> the hardest task in the world!

I must improve my room. I must improve my room. I must improve my room. I must . . . Okay, okay, I get the idea!

Mom says, "When you have a problem, think outside the box."

What box is she talking about? A box of candy? A box of clothes? An empty cardboard box?

My room looks like a box! (A messy, dull, boring one.) Maybe I'll go outside it to think outside it??!

7:48 p.m. Thinking Outside the Box.

1. Backyard. Dark and rainy. I thought

about umbrellas and raincoats and flash-
lights. Ideas for room: Decorate with boots,
raincoats, and umbrellas on wall? Flashlight
theme?

2. Hallway. Tripped on Alex's Rollerblade.
Stared at stain on the wall. Listened to
shower running. Ideas for room: Install
Rollerblading rink? Put in room-sized waterfall?

3. Living room. Sat on couch and
watched TV. Ideas for room: Move into living room and forget about room altogether.

8:30 p.m. I can't think outside the box!!!
Or inside it, either!

8:38 p.m. Went back upstairs. Passed Isabel's room. She was doing her nails
(again). Was too dejected to ask Isabel
how many times she had changed her nail
color today. (She has broken all the world
records in the Hayes Book of World
Records for nail polish use.)

Isabel looked up. "Abby! I want to show you something!"

"What?"

"Come here!"

"Do I have to?"

"Yes!"

"Why?"

"Just come in my room!"

8:39 p.m. Went into Isabel's room. She was sitting at her desk with two trillion bottles of nail polish in front of her.

"That stuff stinks!" I said.

Isabel blew on her nails. "So? I like it."

"It rots your brain."

"Sure it does."

My sister didn't have to defend her beloved nail polish any further. She is the top student in the ninth grade.

"Uh, yeah, right," I mumbled.

"Look, Abby!" Isabel said. She held up her hands and waved them around in the air.

"Huh?"

"My nails, dummy!"

I stared at her nails. They were shiny, wet, and long. They were perfectly manicured. They were oval in shape. They were attached to her fingers. They were—

"Purple!!!!!" I yelled.

"I was wondering when you'd notice."

"They're great," I said.

She held out the bottle of nail polish. "I know you love purple. Do you want purple nails, too?"

"Thanks, Isabel!" I started to open the bottle.

"Take it to your room," Isabel said, pointing to a stack of books on her bed. "I have to study."

8:58 p.m. Went back to room with Isabel's purple nail polish. Painted nails deep, rich, glorious purple. Decided to wear purple shirt, purple barrettes, and purple socks the next day to coordinate.

9:07 p.m. Admired purple fingernails (and purple-spotted fingertips).

9:08 p.m. Looked around my room, then glanced down at purple fingernails.

9:09 p.m. Started to get an idea.

9:10 p.m. Looked around room. Looked down at nails. Looked around room again. Looked down at nails. Looked around room. Looked down at nails.

Kept doing this until I got dizzy.

9:13 p.m. <u>EUREKA!!!!!!!!!!!!!! I have my idea!!!!!!!</u>

9:13½ p.m. Jumped up from chair and leaped around room.

9:15 p.m. Ran into Isabel's room to give her a hug.

9:16 p.m. Ignored Isabel's baffled look. Ran back to room.

9:18 p.m. Admired nails. Looked around room one more time.

9:21 p.m. Counted money in drawer.

9:22 p.m. Put money in pocket of pants I plan to wear tomorrow.

9:26 p.m. Brushed teeth, put on purple pajamas, and climbed into bed.

Sweet dreams!

Chapter 8

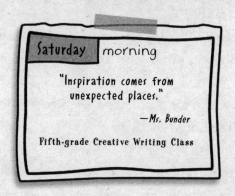

Ms. Bunder is right!

I didn't get my inspiration from inside or outside of a box. It didn't come from thinking. It didn't come from watching television or from standing in the rain in the dark. It came from Isabel's fingernail polish.

(Does Isabel know that her fingernail polish is inspiring? Does she know that big ideas can come from a small bottle?)

Today I am going to buy a can of paint and a paintbrush. Today I am going to paint my lamp purple!!!!

* * *

Other plans:

Buy purple bedspread. (If Mom agrees!)

Find purple lamp shade. (Is there such a thing?)

Display purple toys on shelves. (Must start collection!)

My room will be a Palace of Purple! I will turn it into an awesome, amazing, astonishing, adorable, absolutely Abby abode!

"May I paint my lamp?" Abby asked her mother and father Saturday morning.

Her father raised his eyebrows. "Why not?" he said. "Or rather — why?"

"The last time we painted that lamp was when Isabel and Eva were babies," her mother reminded him. "It was in their nursery."

"The paint is peeling off," Abby said. "It's an ugly yellow."

"Ah," her father said, drinking the rest of his coffee.

"May I paint it?" Abby repeated. "It'll spruce up my room."

"Yes, but only with the windows open!" her father

said. "And lots of newspapers on the floor."

"Newspapers aren't good enough. She should put a drop cloth down," her mother advised. "Or even better, paint it outside."

Abby pointed to the window. "It's raining today. I have to do it in my room."

"We have leftover paint in the garage," her father said. "Odds and ends of blue, green, and yellow. You'll find enough to do a lamp base."

"But I want to paint it purple!" Abby cried.

"Purple?" her father said.

"Purple," Abby said firmly. "It's my favorite color. I want purple in my room."

Her mother nodded as if she understood.

"Do you think I can get purple sheets?" Abby asked her. "Or a purple bedspread?"

"Your bedspread is in good condition," her mother said. "And we have so many sheets. I don't want to buy any more."

Abby's face fell.

"But I'll buy purple cloth and make you new curtains," her mother promised.

"Yay!" Abby said. "Purple curtains!" She flung out her arms. "Mom! You're the greatest! There'll be purple everywhere!"

Her mother shook her head and then smiled.

"I'm going to the hardware store in an hour," her father said. "Will you be ready?"

"Yes!" Abby said.

Abby wandered through aisles of saws, hammers and drills, caulk and sealants, nails and screws, tape measures and plumbing snakes.

"I never knew there were so many tools in the world," she said to her father.

"The paint is over there," her father said. He pointed to a counter stacked high with paint cans. "Pick up some color cards, and find the perfect purple. Then ask for a pint of semigloss paint."

"A pint of semigloss paint," Abby repeated.

"You might even want a high gloss," he said. "Depends on how shiny you'd like it."

Abby looked at her purple fingernails. "About as shiny as these," she said.

"It's your room," her father said.

"Bright purple will perk it up," Abby told him.

"If you say so." He pointed to the other side of the store. "I'll be there if you need me. I've got a dozen things to buy."

"Okay. Thanks, Dad!" Abby said.

She headed over to the paint section.

"Where are the color cards?" she asked the woman behind the counter.

"Over there," she said.

"Do you have lots of purples?" she asked.

"Oh, yes!" the woman said.

She was right. There were rows of color cards with every shade imaginable. Abby pulled out six and compared the color chips to her fingernails.

"Do you need any help?" The woman followed her to the color card display. "I can show you what we have. Or you can browse on your own."

"I'm trying to find this color purple," Abby said, pointing to her nail polish.

"We've never had anyone match paint to nail polish before," the woman commented. She took the color cards from Abby and quickly looked through them.

"This one," she said. "Or this. It depends whether you like a redder purple or a bluer one."

"I like this one," Abby said. She read its name out loud. "The People's Purple."

"That's a strange color name," the woman said. "Sometimes I wonder who thinks up all those names."

"I'd call it Jumping for Joy," Abby said. That was how the color made her feel.

"That's a better one," the woman said. "Maybe you should go to work for the paint company."

Abby smiled. "I could think of hundreds of names for purple!" she cried. "Jumping for Joy, Particularly Purple, Great Grape, Purple Majesty . . ."

The woman led her to the cash register. "How much People's Purple do you need?" she asked. "And do you want flat, semigloss, or gloss?"

"I'm painting a lamp," Abby told her. "I might paint my desk and bureau, too."

"I'd take a gallon of either semigloss or gloss," the woman advised. "We have a sale right now, and you can get two gallons for the price of one."

"I'll take a gallon of the gloss," Abby said. "I mean, two."

With two gallons for the price of one, she'd have the People's Purple on hand for any purple project she could dream of. She could paint her chair, her bookcase, or her bed. Wait until her friends saw! They would be so impressed with her room!

"That'll be twenty-one ninety-five," the woman said. She hauled two gallons of the People's Purple onto the counter. "Here's a mixing stick, too. Do you need paintbrushes or rollers or drop cloths?"

"We have them at home," Abby said. She counted out the dollar bills in her pocket.

Her father came up next to her at the counter.

"I'll pay for that," he said.

"You will? Thanks, Dad!"

"Where's that pint of paint?" he asked, pulling out his wallet.

"I got two gallons." Abby pointed to the cans on the counter.

"Two *gallons*?" her father cried. "You don't need that much!"

"It's on sale, Dad!"

"No, Abby."

"But Dad," Abby protested, "I need at least a gallon. I might paint my desk and chair!"

"It's a two-for-one special," the woman explained. "You might as well take the extra gallon. It's free."

Her father shook his head. "We don't need two gallons of the People's Purple!"

"What if I decide to paint the old wicker chairs in the backyard?" Abby asked. "I might want purple lawn furniture for my party!"

"That's a lot of painting, Abby. It's hard work. You'll probably be fed up with painting by the time you've finished the lamp."

"No," Abby insisted, "I won't be."

"Abby," her father said, "I have more experience in this than you."

"The sale ends tomorrow," the woman informed them.

Abby took a breath. "All right, I'll pay for the two gallons myself! It's my money, and I can decide what to do with it."

She laid twenty-two dollars on the counter.

The saleswoman looked at her father. "That's it, then?" she said. "You're taking the two gallons?"

"Yes!" Abby said.

"All right," her father said. He put his wallet back in his pocket. "If it's your money!"

The woman put a paid sticker on the cans of paint. "Here you are. Good luck with your project!"

Abby's father picked up the paint. They went out to the car.

Paul Hayes put the key in the ignition. He fastened his seat belt. He sighed and tapped his fingers on the steering wheel.

Suddenly, he turned toward Abby.

"Let's make a deal," he said. "I'll pay for half of the paint." He reached into his pocket, pulled out his wallet, and counted out eleven dollars.

"Really?" Abby said.

"I said I'd pay," he said. "I don't want to go back on my word."

Abby flung her arms around her father.

"You won't be sorry!" she promised. "My room will be the most beautiful you've ever seen!"

Chapter 9

Sunday | early

"You should not paint the
chair, but only what
someone has felt about it."

—Edvard Munch

Lawn Furniture Calendar

What have I felt about my lamp?

1. It gives me light so I can read and write in my journal. (Thanks, lamp.)

2. It sits on my desk. (Hi.)

3. It is an ugly yellow. (Can't wait until it's rich, shiny purple!)

What about my other furniture?

1. It's in my room. (Hooray.)

2. It's white, brown, and faded blue. (Ho-hum.)

3. It is useful. (Surprise!)

No, I don't want to paint what I feel. I want to feel great after I've painted!

Paintbrush in hand, Abby surveyed her room.

She had protected her furniture and floor with drop cloths, old sheets, and newspapers. Good thing. There were drips, splatters, and brush marks everywhere!

Abby herself was covered with purple. Her old jeans and ripped-up T-shirt were smudged and smeared. Her cheek had a streak of purple on it. Her red hair now had purple highlights.

She and the room looked like a purple cyclone had passed through.

The lamp, however, had turned out beautifully. It was wet, shiny, and perfectly purple.

It looked better than Abby had ever imagined. Her whole room seemed transformed already, just by painting one lamp!

She took off the sheet covering the desk. It had once belonged to Eva. A long time ago, her father had painted it blue. An earlier green coat showed through in spots.

For a moment, she stood staring at it.

The lamp had been tricky to paint because of its curves. She had managed with a small brush and slow, steady brush strokes. The desk would be easier. It was flat and rectangular. There was only one drawer.

What would it be like to have a purple desk with a purple lamp sitting on it?

"The ultimate in purpleness," Abby said out loud. Finally, she would have a room that would shout Abby!

She stirred the paint in its can. Then she dipped a large brush in the paint and held it poised above the desk.

"Are you ready, desk?" She began to brush the deep, rich purple paint onto the desk with long, smooth strokes.

Abby pulled out the desk drawer, placed it on some newspapers, and painted it carefully. Then she painted the sides and the back of the desk, making sure not to leave any drips or bare spots.

She rested the brush on the top of the paint can and stood back to admire her handiwork.

It looked good. Okay, it looked great. She *loved* it! Her room was improved a million times over. She was probably the only girl in the fifth grade with hand-painted purple furniture!

There was a knock on the door.

"What are you painting?" Eva asked.

Isabel pinched her nose. "We can smell the fumes all the way down the hall. You think nail polish stinks? This is worse!"

"I think it smells good," Abby began, when her sisters interrupted her.

"WOW!" Isabel shrieked. "It looks *great*!"

"I love it!" Eva cried.

"Really?" Abby said. "You like it?"

"You did a terrific job," Isabel said admiringly. "No drips or glops or anything."

"I wanted to make my room unique and unforgettable," Abby explained.

"You have," Eva assured her.

"No one will ever forget your room," Isabel agreed.

Abby shook her head. Her twin sisters never praised her like this. They never even agreed!

"I might show it to my friends during the party," she confided.

"Speaking of the party," Isabel began.

"What have you planned so far?" Eva finished. "Have you thought about games? Decorations? Food?"

"Everything is organized and ready to go," Abby said. "We're eating hot dogs, chips, popcorn, potato salad, watermelon, ice cream, and cake. I wrote down games to play. Could you lend me some CDs and your CD player?"

Isabel nodded.

"Who's making the food?" Eva asked. "Who's doing the shopping? Who's baking the cakes?"

"If you want, Eva and I will help you make the cakes," Isabel offered in a friendly way.

"Um — " Abby hesitated. She had had enough of Eva and Isabel's "help" with the invitations.

"For fifty kids, you're going to need a couple of big sheet cakes," Eva said. "You also need to buy paper plates and plastic silverware. And what about drinks?"

"Oh, yeah," Abby said. "I forgot about drinks."

"You can't forget, Abby. Especially when fifty kids are running around getting thirsty." Isabel shook her head. "How many kids are actually coming?"

"Almost everyone," Abby said. She crossed her fingers. "Except Brianna and Victoria — I hope."

"They're both a pain," Eva agreed.

"If fifty kids show up," Isabel said, "you definitely need Eva and me. We'll be your own personal party consultants. Right, Eva?"

"Right, Isabel."

Abby stared at them. It wasn't very often that she saw her twin sisters agreeing like this. Had their brains been affected by the purple paint? Was it the fumes or the color?

"We'll be in charge of activities," Isabel continued.

"But shouldn't a party be like recess?" Abby cried. "Everyone can amuse themselves!"

"You're asking for trouble with that many kids," Eva said.

"We have experience," Isabel told her. "And lots of ideas."

"If you paint my desk for me," Eva said, "I'll give you all the help you want."

"Well . . ." Abby began. "Maybe."

"I'll do it for free," Isabel said, with a meaningful glance at her twin. "I don't sell my services to my little sister!"

Eva shot her a dirty look. "It's called barter!" she snapped. "There's nothing wrong with it!"

"I love painting," Abby said, trying to change the

subject. "Maybe when I'm older, I'll get a job painting houses. Don't you think I'd be good at it?"

"*Yes*," Eva and Isabel said at the same time.

"Think about our offer," Isabel said.

"I will," Abby promised. She'd attend to the party details soon. Right now, she had something more important on her mind: her room.

Abby's twin sisters walked around the desk and lamp again.

"I love them!" Eva said again. "They're *so* fantastic!"

"Amazing," Isabel said.

"Purple splendor!" Abby said.

"That's a good name for a color," Eva said.

"Purple splendor," Abby repeated as Eva and Isabel went out the door. The words rolled off her tongue like music.

She was on a roll. Or maybe a roller. She picked up a paint roller and held it up. What could she paint next? She had barely used up any of the paint. There were almost two full gallons left!

If Abby's room looked great with a purple desk and lamp, imagine what it would look like if *everything* was purple!

Where should she start?

The bureau? Too many drawers. The chair? Too many curvy parts. The bookcase? Too many books and toys to unpack.

For a moment, Abby studied her room. She leaned down and poured a little paint into the paint tray. She moved the roller back and forth to coat it with glossy purple paint. Then she rolled it out onto an empty section of her wall.

Chapter 10

Sunday | later

"My eyes have seen what
my hand did."

—Robert Lowell

Stitch and Mend Calendar

<u>What my hand did:</u>
Painted the walls of my
room glossy purple.
Painted the bookcase.
(Ran out of paint or I
would have done the bureau and chair, too.)

<u>What my eyes have seen:</u>
Purple, purple everywhere! My room is a
sea of shining purple!

My walls are <u>very</u> purple.
It's like being inside a grape
or a giant purple box.

* * *

I will put my room in the <u>Hayes Book of World Records</u> for "Purplest Possible Painted Space" and "Totally Terrific Transformation of Practically Pathetic Room."

I love it! I love it! I <u>love</u> it!

<u>What my hand still has to do</u>:
Clean up!!!!

Wash the brushes and rollers.
Put away paint trays and stack empty cans of paint in the garage.
Throw out newspapers and fold up sheets and drop cloths.
Take a shower and change my clothes.

<u>What my eyes still want to see</u>:
My family's reaction when they walk into the Palace of Purple!

Will they jump up and down from excitement?
Will they want their own purple rooms?

Will they decide to paint the entire house purple?

Will I be able to have a purple party?

(Note: Ask Mom if I can buy purple plates, purple cups, purple napkins, purple prizes, and purple iced cake. Too bad I didn't think of asking all the fifth-graders to come dressed in purple!)

It's almost dinnertime. I will give my family a tour after dessert.

The Purple Play
by Abby Hayes

Setting: A purple bedroom
Characters: the Hayes family: Paul, Olivia, Eva, Isabel, Alex, and Abby
Time: Sunday after dinner

As the play opens, Abby Hayes, a ten-year-old girl with curly red hair (and a few purple streaks), leads her family up-stairs to her bedroom.

* * *

Eva: You won't believe it, Mom and Dad!

Isabel: What else did you do, Abby?

Abby (mysteriously): Oh, this and that.

Olivia Hayes: I can't wait to see it!

Paul Hayes: You used up two gallons of paint. I'm impressed. Are you sure you didn't pour it down the drain?

Abby: Ha-ha. Very funny.

Alex: Can I paint _my_ lamp, too?

Paul Hayes (groans): See what you've started?

Abby: A purple riot?

Olivia Hayes: You even cleaned up after yourself.

Abby: Yep.

The Hayes family reaches the top of the stairs. With a triumphant smile, Abby flings open the door to her room.

Abby: EXPERIENCE THE PURPLE!

Mouths fall open. Eyes glaze over. Hands fly to throats. The Hayes family gapes at the walls and furniture.

For the first time in recorded history, both Isabel <u>and</u> Eva are speechless.

The silence lasts for several minutes. It is finally broken by Olivia Hayes.

Olivia Hayes: Your room is so, so . . . <u>purple</u>!

Paul Hayes: The People's Purple packs a punch.

Eva: Wow. Wow. Wow.

Isabel (is having trouble breathing): Oh! It looks like you painted your walls with fingernail polish!

Abby: Exactly.

Alex: Cool! Awesome! Cool!

Olivia Hayes frowns. Paul Hayes rubs the stubble on his cheek. The Hayes parents appear to be worried.

Abby: Isn't it <u>great</u>, Mom and Dad?

Olivia Hayes: How many coats will it take to repaint it?

Paul Hayes: Probably six.

Olivia Hayes: We could tack bedsheets on the walls.

Paul Hayes: Or wallpaper it.

Olivia Hayes: How about pine panels?

Abby: Wait a minute! I don't want to change a thing! I <u>love</u> my purple room!!!

Paul Hayes: In one week, you'll be begging for white walls.

Abby: I <u>won't</u>!

Olivia Hayes: You don't want a calm, gentle, restful shade of lilac?

Abby: No!

Paul Hayes: Can you really live with this, Abby?

Abby: Of course!

The Hayes parents turn to each other and shrug.

Olivia Hayes: It's her room, isn't it?

Paul Hayes: When she gets sick of it, she'll just have to repaint it.

Olivia Hayes: What about curtains, Abby? I hope you've changed your mind. You have enough purple in your room now.

Abby: No! There's <u>never</u> enough purple! The more, the merrier!

The play ends as Eva, Isabel, and Alex cluster around Abby, asking her to paint <u>their</u> rooms!

PURPLE PAINT FOREVER!!!!!

I am going to call all my friends and tell them.

No, I'll surprise them.

Chapter 11

Thursday

"I never think of the future. It comes soon enough."

—*Albert Einstein*

Great Big Calendar of Time and Space

He's right!!!!!

The future is far away.

The present is right now.

I'm thinking about the present, not the future.

<u>The Present</u>:

My room is magnificently purple. Last night I painted my bureau and chair with more of the People's Purple paint. Mom is making curtains for me. They are pale lilac

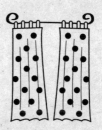

with purple polka dots. She also gave me a purple-patterned bedspread. Why should I think about the future when my present is perfectly purple???

(Note: How many "p" words did I use in the last paragraph? Purple, painted, People's, Purple, paint, pale, purple, polka dots, purple-patterned, present, perfectly, purple. If you can say that seven times very quickly without stumbling, you will win a page in the Hayes Book of World Records!)

The Future:

Eva and Isabel want me to think about the future. The future is my party. They want me to plan and prepare everything in advance. I still have more than a week to go!!! I already did some of the stuff.

Mom and I bought plastic forks, spoons, and knives, plates, napkins, and cups. We also bought ten bottles of soda and party prizes. Yes, the prizes are pencils.

So there, Eva and Isabel! I am preparing! (And adding more "p" words: Party, plan, prepare, plastic, plates, prizes, and pencils!!!)

If I listened to my "wise, experienced" twin sisters, I'd worry about the future every single second. I'm going to enjoy my perfectly purple room instead!!!!!!

Last night I hung my calendars on the walls. The pictures of animals, sunsets, oceans, and vegetables really stand out now! My calendars look exciting in my newly painted room!

"I have your essays about your rooms," Ms. Bunder announced to the fifth-graders. She held up a sheaf of papers. "I reread every single one."

Abby's stomach lurched. The room essay hadn't been one of her best. In fact, it might have been one of her worst. It had been difficult to find *anything* to say about her room last week.

Tyler raised his hand. "Why did you have to read them again? We read them out loud in class!!!"

Ms. Bunder nodded. "Reading to yourself is a different experience from having a paper read to you. Sometimes a student will mutter and swallow the words. I'll miss hearing the best parts. It can work the other way around, too. Sometimes a student with dramatic flair will give life to a poorly written piece."

Abby wondered if she had done that. Had Ms. Bunder looked at her assignment and realized it was even worse than she thought?

"Get out your writing notebooks," Ms. Bunder instructed the students. "I'll return last week's work, and then we'll get started on something new."

She went from desk to desk, handing students their papers.

"I got an A+!" Bethany squealed.

"For writing about *hamsters*?" Brianna demanded.

"It's not *what* you write about, it's *how* you write about it," Ms. Bunder told her, loud enough so the entire class could hear.

"That's not always true," Abby whispered to Natalie. "My room was boring so I wrote a boring essay about it."

Natalie shook her head. "You're wrong. I liked your essay."

Abby shrugged. Natalie was a loyal friend. But *she* was the one who was wrong.

Ms. Bunder handed Brianna her paper. "Not bad, Brianna."

"Not bad?" Brianna repeated in disbelief. She glanced at her paper. Her face turned red.

"Ms. Bunder! I deserve better than a B!" she cried. "No one else in the fifth grade has a large-screen television in their bedroom!"

"Brianna, I'm not grading you on equipment," Ms. Bunder said.

"Why not?" Brianna demanded.

Ms. Bunder ignored her.

"Hey, look at this!" Mason yelled, pointing to his paper. Ms. Bunder had marked it with a large A.

"Congratulations," Abby said. Mason had an A; Bethany had an A+; Brianna had a B. Was this going to be Abby's first C in creative writing?

Abby wanted to jump up and tell everyone that her room was now completely transformed; that she had sanded and scraped and painted all weekend; and that she now had a purple lamp, bureau, chair, bookcase, and curtains.

But she wanted to surprise her friends, too. She didn't want to give away her secret before she figured out the perfect way to reveal it.

"Abby," Ms. Bunder said. "Here you go."

Abby flipped the paper over fast before she could see the grade. "I can't look," she said to Natalie.

"You tell me what it is."

Natalie turned the paper over. "B+," she announced.

"Really?"

"B+," Natalie repeated firmly.

Abby opened her eyes. She looked down at her paper. "Wow!" she cried. "B+! That's *good*."

"I told you!" Natalie said. " 'It's not what you write about, it's how you write about it,' " she repeated.

"It's better than I thought," Abby said. She leaned toward Natalie.

Abby *had* to tell *someone* about her room. "Guess what," she began.

"What?" Natalie asked.

Ms. Bunder clapped her hands for the students' attention. She picked up a piece of chalk. "Who has ever written a What I Did on My Summer Vacation essay?" she asked.

"It's nothing," Abby whispered to Natalie as the entire class raised their hands. "I'll tell you later."

Ms. Bunder smiled. "Today we'll write something a little different. We'll write a What I'd *Like* to Do on My Summer Vacation essay."

"Huh?" Mason said.

"If you could do *anything*," Ms. Bunder explained, "what would you do on summer vacation?"

"Read joke books," Rachel said.

"Camp out under the stars for three months!" Jessica said.

"Work in an animal hospital!" Bethany cried.

Dozens of voices broke out at once.

"I want to go swimming!" "Visit my cousins!" "Watch a lot of TV!" "Go to Paris!" "Do nothing!"

Ms. Bunder held up her hand for quiet. "The sky's the limit," she said. "Write about how you would spend an ideal summer vacation. It doesn't matter if it's on Mars or at the New Jersey shore."

Abby and Natalie exchanged glances.

"Hogwarts," Natalie said. She grabbed a pen and paper.

"Nonstop computer games!" Zach yelled.

"Write it down," Ms. Bunder instructed. "How would it feel to play computer games all day and all night? Is that *really* your ideal summer vacation?"

Abby looked down at the blank paper. No ideas came to mind. She silently reread the ending to her last week's assignment.

"I wish I had a purple billowy ceiling! I wish I had a purple rug and purple curtains! I wish I could turn my room into a Palace of Purple!"

A week ago, this had been just a dream. Now it was reality.

I did it, she said to herself. *I really DID turn my room into a Palace of Purple! And got a B+ on an essay that I didn't think was very good.*

If she imagined something wonderful for her summer vacation, would it really happen?

Now that she had transformed her room, what was left?

Abby thought. She might attend a writer's workshop for kids. Throw the best party that the fifth grade had ever seen. Go on an airplane by herself and visit Grandma Emma. Learn to play the piano.

That was just the beginning.

She picked up her pen and began to write.

Chapter 12

I wish it did! I'd love to have time work wonders. It would be great if time shopped for my party, made the food, put up the decorations, and chose the music. How can I get time to do that?

I need <u>someone</u> to work wonders! I've been so busy thinking about my room, I haven't even thought about my party.

The party is tomorrow! Fifty-one kids are showing up. Everyone is coming, even Brianna and Victoria.

(We pause for a moment of silent screaming.)

* * *

I'm not ready. I'm not even close to ready. What about food? What about tables? What about games? What about decorations? And music? Time isn't helping at all! It's bringing me closer and closer to my party.

Eva and Isabel were right. I should have prepared in advance. I should have accepted their help. Is it too late? Will they still help me?

Abby slammed her journal shut, jumped up from her bed, and went to find her father.

"Dad!" she called, running up the stairs to his home office. "Are you there?"

He didn't answer. No one else was home. Her mother was still at work. Her twin sisters were still at school. Eva had lacrosse practice; Isabel had drama club. Alex was at a friend's house.

"Dad!" Abby yelled. *"Dad!"*

"I'm here!" Paul Hayes appeared at the bottom of the stairs. "What's the matter, Abby? You sound desperate!"

"I am! My party is tomorrow!" Abby wailed.

"Nothing's ready! Except my room," she added. "I should have had everything done by now!"

"Calm down," her father said. "You're not in this alone. No one expects you to throw a party for the entire fifth grade by yourself. Your mother and I haven't forgotten that fifty-one hungry ten-year-olds will descend on the house tomorrow at two P.M. No way!"

Paul Hayes took a piece of paper out of his pocket. He unfolded it and began to read. "Twenty packages of hot dogs and rolls, ten bags of chips, popcorn, three gallons of ice cream, a bucket of potato salad, six bottles of juice, five watermelons . . ."

He looked at Abby. "That's the shopping list. All right?"

Abby nodded.

Her father continued. "We'll go shopping after dinner. While we're at the supermarket, your mother will haul out the tables, the tent, bowls, and serving utensils. Your sisters are baking the cakes."

"*Together?*" Abby cried in dismay.

"Even the twins occasionally cooperate," Paul Hayes said. "Though I admit I haven't seen it often."

"What if they start fighting and burn the cake?

What if they forget to put in baking powder? What if they use salt instead of sugar?"

"If you're that worried, why don't you bake the cakes?" her father suggested. "You'll have to do it after shopping, decorating, and setting up tables."

"Eva and Isabel can bake them!" Abby said quickly. "I just hope they don't ruin everything!"

"It'll turn out fine," her father reassured her. "You can count on your sisters to bake two delicious cakes."

"Tasting is believing," Abby muttered.

Her father put his hand on her shoulder. "What do you have left to do?"

"Just decorating, blowing up balloons, finding music, planning a few games, making sure everyone has a good time, and cleaning up afterward."

"You'll get through it," her father promised. "So will we."

Abby unloaded the groceries from the car.

"Did you and your dad get everything?" her mother asked, pushing back a stray lock of hair from her face. She was pulling serving utensils out of a drawer.

"Yes," Abby said.

"Eggs?" Isabel asked. "Cream cheese? Confectioner's sugar? Eva and I need them for the frostings."

"I think so," Abby said. She rummaged in one of the bags and pulled out a carton of eggs and a package of cream cheese. "Here's some of it, anyway. What are you making?"

"I'm making a carrot cake with cream cheese frosting," Eva announced, pointing to a stainless steel bowl full of batter. "And Isabel is making a double chocolate cake with creamy vanilla frosting."

"Yum!" Abby said. "Can I lick the bowls?"

"No way!" Isabel said. "Get out of here! Don't disturb the chefs!"

"Here, Abby." Eva poured the batter into a large pan, then scraped the bowl with a spatula that she offered to her younger sister. "You can taste this."

"Don't!" Isabel warned. "You might get sick from the raw eggs!"

Abby hesitated.

"You don't want to be ill the night before your party," her mother agreed. "Put that in the dishwasher, Eva."

"I licked it," Eva said. "It's delicious."

"If you throw up all night and have a fever,

don't expect any sympathy from me," Isabel said.

"I never expect any sympathy from you, anyway," Eva retorted. She held out the spatula to Abby. "Sure you don't want a taste?"

Abby shook her head. "I don't think so." She put the packages of hot dogs into the refrigerator. The last thing she needed was food poisoning.

Eva put the pan into the oven. "Only one hour, and the carrot cake will be ready!" she announced.

"Hooray!" Abby said.

Isabel was emptying her bowl into another pan. "This is going to be the best chocolate cake you've ever tasted," she promised Abby. "Do you know what the secret is?"

"What?" Abby asked. "Coconut? Orange flavoring? Cherries?"

"Vinegar," Isabel announced.

"Vinegar?" Abby cried. "Are you crazy?"

"Nope," Isabel said, sliding the pan into the oven and setting the timer. "This cake will be delicious."

"Mom! She'll ruin my party!" Abby cried. "Do something!"

"She'll ruin it," Eva agreed. "Isabel ruins everything."

Isabel stuck her tongue out at her twin.

Olivia Hayes paused at the sink, where she was

filling ice cube trays with water. "Stop it, Eva and Isabel. Stop tormenting your sister." She turned to Abby. "It's a perfectly good recipe. I've made it many times myself. The cake is excellent."

"Are you *sure*?" Abby asked anxiously. Vinegar cake sounded like a nightmare. She could already see her friends and classmates puckering up.

"If it isn't, I'll get a cake from the bakery," her mother promised. "Now let's set up the folding tables on the back porch."

Alex ran into the kitchen in his pajamas. "I want to help, too! Can I bake a cake?"

"They're already done," Eva said, affectionately ruffling his hair.

"They smell good," Alex said.

Abby looked in one of the bags. "Alex! Do you want to blow up some balloons?" she asked him. "I'm going to tie them on the back porch and fence."

Alex nodded his head.

"Here." Abby handed him a package of purple balloons. "Be sure to tie them tight so the air won't leak out," she instructed him.

"I *know*!" Alex said.

Abby followed her mother onto the back porch. Together they set up the folding tables.

"We'll put tablecloths on them tomorrow," her mother said. "We don't want them blowing away overnight."

"No!" Abby agreed. She already had vinegar cake. She didn't want runaway tablecloths, too.

She looked up at the sky. It was filled with clouds. Another thing to worry about. "What if the weather's bad?" she asked. "What if it's cold or pouring?"

Olivia Hayes shook her head. "I'm rooting for blue skies. If we have fifty kids in the house . . ." Her voice trailed off.

"We could go down to the basement," Abby suggested. "We could rent movies and play Ping-Pong."

"The basement will hold twenty people, maximum," her mother said. "We'd have to divide the party. Put half in the living room and half downstairs."

"And some in my room!" Abby said.

Her mother frowned. "I don't want the entire fifth grade running wild in the house. We better keep our fingers crossed."

"Okay," Abby said. "I'll cross my toes, too."

The smell of freshly baked cakes filled the house. Eva and Isabel were preparing frostings as the sheet cakes cooled on the countertops.

"My cream cheese frosting is a lot healthier than yours," Eva said, casting a critical eye on Isabel's bowl. "Yours is all sugar."

"Guess whose cake is going to be the most popular?" Isabel retorted.

"Just don't tell anyone the ingredients!" Eva said.

"No one will know," Isabel said. "And everyone will want seconds!"

"I hope so," Abby said, coming into the kitchen with Alex, who was still blowing up balloons.

"Don't worry," her father said. He was carrying bags of charcoal and a grill for the hot dogs.

Abby looked around at the kitchen. The sink was filled with bowls. The table was stacked with party food and utensils. A few stray balloons lay on the floor. There were to-do lists on the refrigerator and dirty forks and spoons on the countertops.

"That's all anyone says!" she cried. "Don't worry! Don't worry! Why should I stop worrying? The entire fifth grade will be here tomorrow!"

"She has party panic," Isabel said, stirring the frosting with a spoon.

"Wait until you've thrown four or five parties in a row," Eva said. "It'll get a lot easier."

Her father set down the charcoal and grill by the

back door. "I told you, Abby. You're not alone. You've got plenty of people helping you."

Alex knotted a string on a purple balloon to tie on the front door. "Yeah, Abby," he agreed. "Like me."

Her father dusted off his hands. "We'll give you more help tomorrow."

Abby took a deep breath. "You're right, Dad," she said, looking around at her family. "Thanks, every-one!"

"We'll make you pay later," Eva joked.

"Yeah, wait until *our* next party," Isabel said.

In her room, Abby lay back on her bed and gazed at her purple walls. She sighed with satisfaction, then reached for her journal and opened it up.

Time didn't work wonders, but my family did!

Hayes Family Wonder Workers:

1. Dad. Bought food, set up grill, will make hot dogs tomorrow.

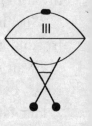

2. Mom. Got out folding tables. Took out tablecloths. Stacked paper plates, plastic silverware,

napkins, and cups on tables. Made extra
ice cubes. Got out serving utensils, juice
pitchers, and cutting boards. Found crepe
paper for decorations.

      3. Isabel. Baked chocolate
(vinegar) cake and frosted it.
      4. Eva. Baked carrot cake and
frosted it. Wrote "Hooray! It's Summer!" on both cakes in purple icing.
      5. Alex. Blew up one package of
purple balloons. Tied balloon to front door
so friends can find party.
  6. Abby. Thought of party. Won argument
with parents. Planned and printed invitations. Painted room purple. Went shopping
with Dad. Put away food. Helped Mom
carry out tables. Drew stars, hearts, and
squiggles on both cakes to decorate. Blew
up some balloons.

 Are we ready? Almost!!!!!!!!

Chapter 13

Saturday

"Tomorrow never comes."

Calendar of Days

Yes, it does! Tomorrow is here! It's today!

Today is my party. Soon my classmates will be here!

HOORAY!!!

Abby looked out the front window. "When will they arrive?" she asked impatiently.

Isabel smiled. "Not for at least another ten minutes," she said. "And people usually come late, anyway."

The tables were set up for the party. There were

platters of cheese and rolls and fruit. There were bowls of popcorn and gallons of soda. The cakes were iced and decorated and hidden in the refrigerator.

The yard was ready, too. Alex had plugged in the boom box and stacked a pile of CDs next to it. The volleyball net stretched across the back of the yard. Abby had dragged out a trunk full of games. There were balloons tied to the fence and the back porch.

Abby walked over to the mirror and stared anxiously at her reflection. She was wearing a purple T-shirt and purple-flowered pants. There were purple barrettes in her hair, and she wore sneakers with purple daisies.

"You look cute," Isabel said. "Are you going to show everyone your purple room?"

Abby shook her head. "No."

She had decided to invite Jessica, Natalie, and Bethany — and maybe Casey — to see it at the end of the party. "Only my close friends."

A car door slammed. There were footsteps on the front porch.

"Someone's here," Isabel said just as the doorbell rang.

Abby ran to answer it. "It's Jessica and Sarah!" she cried. "You're our first guests!"

Jessica handed her a platter of cookies. "These are for the party," she said. "My mother and I made them this morning."

"Thanks!" Abby said.

Sarah shifted uncomfortably on the front steps. "I didn't bring anything," she said. "I hope that's okay."

"We have *plenty* of food," Abby told her.

"Wait until you taste my chocolate cake!" Isabel called.

"Great!" Jessica said.

"It better be," Abby said under her breath.

"What?" Sarah asked.

Abby didn't answer. "The party's in the backyard," she said instead. "I'll show you the way."

"I *know* where it is!" Jessica reminded her. "I've only been here a million times since kindergarten."

"Oh, yeah, right," Abby said.

"If you want to go out back with your friends, I'll answer the bell," Isabel offered.

"Thanks, sis," Abby said. She led her friends through the house.

The entire fifth grade of Lancaster Elementary was gathered in the Hayes backyard.

The boys stood on one side. The girls stood on the other.

Led by Mason, the boys were having a burping contest. Tyler was burping the alphabet. Zach was cheering him on. Casey was claiming he could burp "Twinkle, Twinkle" and "When You Wish Upon a Star." Jonathan was betting he couldn't.

The girls were clustered around Brianna and Victoria, who were describing the Tiffany Crystal concert the night before.

"We had front-row seats," Brianna bragged. "My cousin got us the best tickets. Right, Bethany?"

Bethany was silent.

"Too bad you couldn't come," Victoria snickered.

"I only had two tickets," Brianna explained. "Of *course* I had to give one to Victoria. You understand, don't you, Bethany?"

"Well, actually, I — " Bethany began.

"Who cares?" Victoria interrupted. "The concert was great. I got, like, tons of cool stuff. A poster, two new CDs — "

"I bought an authentic Tiffany Crystal key chain," Brianna bragged.

"I don't — " Bethany tried to say.

"Tiffany Crystal was, like, totally awesome," Victoria continued. "The singing and dancing were the best. I, like, *love* her song "Nasty Sugar Sweet — "

Brianna and Victoria linked arms and burst into song.

"Someone shut them up," Natalie moaned. "Please!"

"I'll do it!" Abby's little brother Alex offered. He scampered onto the porch, put a CD in the boom box, and turned the volume up full blast.

Victoria and Brianna broke off their singing.

"Like, *what*?" Victoria said.

"The Bumble Boys!" Brianna cried. "Are you serious?"

"They're the bomb," Alex said.

"I, like, totally hate the Bumble Boys," Victoria said. "Can you put on some Tiffany Crystal?"

"Sorry," Abby said, "I don't have any Tiffany."

"This is a Tiffany-free zone," Natalie said.

Victoria rolled her eyes. "Why am I, like, here, instead of at the mall?"

Brianna cast a quick glance in the direction of the boys. Mason let out an enormous burp.

"They are so immature!" Brianna shrieked. "Why didn't you take my advice, Abby, and invite the sixth- and seventh-grade boys instead?"

"Eeeeuuu!" Rachel said. "They're even *worse*!"

"No, they're not," Brianna disagreed.

"Boys are boring," Bethany said suddenly in a loud voice. "I like hamsters better. Sometimes I like them better than girls, too."

Everyone stared at her.

"What?" Tyler yelled. "She prefers hamsters to people?"

"She *lives* in a hamster cage," Victoria said nastily.

Bethany's eyes widened. Her face got red. Her lip wobbled.

"My room doesn't smell," Victoria sneered.

"Blondie doesn't smell any worse than you or Brianna!" Bethany retorted.

There was a moment of shocked silence. Then suddenly everyone was arguing.

Tyler and Zach were yelling that girls were worse than boys. Rachel and Natalie were yelling that boys were worse than girls. Victoria was yelling at Brianna that it was time to leave the party. Brianna was yelling at Bethany that it was her fault. Bethany was yelling that she hated Victoria. Mason was burping. Jonathan and Megan were high-fiving each other, although no one knew why. Sarah and Jessica yelled for someone to turn down the music.

The Bumble Boys were blaring.

The Hayes backyard was a scene of pandemonium.

Abby looked around frantically for help. Isabel and Eva were nowhere in sight. Alex was fiddling with the CD player, turning the volume up and down. Her parents were getting food from the kitchen.

"Stop! Stop, everyone!" Abby cried wildly. She ran from one person to another, trying to get them to stop fighting.

No one listened.

As suddenly as it had begun, the fight ended. Bethany wiped the tears from her eyes and started to shoot hoops with Jessica and Sarah. A group of boys and girls went over to the volleyball net. Brianna reapplied colored lip gloss.

"At least there's music," Victoria grumbled. She began to dance to the music of the Bumble Boys.

Paul and Olivia Hayes came out of the house with a big bowl of potato salad and packages of hot dogs. Abby's father fired up the grill.

"Nice party, honey," he said to Abby. "Everyone's having a good time."

"Uh, yeah," Abby said. "Sure, Dad."

The fifth-graders had just finished eating hot dogs, potato salad, chips, and watermelon when Isabel and Eva carried out the cakes.

"Happy end of school year to you!" they sang. "Happy end of school year to you! Have a great summer vacation — and eat lots of cake, too!"

Abby's twin sisters set the cakes down on a table.

"This is my extraordinary carrot cake with cream cheese icing," Eva announced.

"And this is my fabulous chocolate cake with vanilla icing," Isabel said. "With the mystery ingredient."

She picked up a toy horn and tooted on it.

"We are now serving cake," the twins announced in unison.

The fifth-graders rushed toward the tables.

Abby took a piece of Eva's cake and a piece of Isabel's. With her fork, she pried loose a tiny crumb of Isabel's mystery chocolate cake. Carefully, she put it in her mouth. She closed her eyes and tasted.

"It's good!" she said in surprise.

"*Told* you!" Isabel smirked.

"Have you tasted mine?" Eva demanded. "It's even better!"

Abby took a large forkful of carrot cake. "It's delicious, too!"

"They're both great," Jessica agreed.

"Yuh," Casey agreed, his mouth full of cake.

"I wish this party would never end!" Natalie said.

"Me, too," Jonathan agreed.

"Can I have second helpings?" Tyler asked.

"What about thirds?" Mason demanded.

Victoria made a face. "Piggy, piggy."

"This cake is good, but the cake my mother ordered from the French bakery was even better," Brianna said. *"Eh bien, c'est vrai, n'est-ce pas?"*

"Speak English!" Natalie said. "No one understands a word you're saying!"

"Thank goodness," Abby said under her breath.

Bethany snickered.

"Tant pis," Brianna said. "Too bad. If you're all ignorant — " She stood up to throw out her paper plate.

"Another game of volleyball?" Abby suggested.

"Great idea! Yeah! Let's do it!" Her classmates got up and ran over to the net.

The party was going as smoothly as possible, Abby thought with satisfaction. The games were fun, the food was great — even the vinegar cake! — and all the fifth-graders were laughing and having a good time.

Abby hadn't needed Isabel and Eva's party-planning services, after all. She was just a natural party-giver.

She picked up the volleyball and served it over the net.

"Eeeeeeeeeee!" The first shriek came from Brianna.

"Aaaaaaaaaaa!" The second came from Victoria.

Fat, wet, purple water balloons were exploding in front of the two best-dressed girls in the fifth grade.

They flung their arms up to protect themselves, but they were already drenched from head to toe. Their sequined scoop-necked T-shirts, shiny short skirts, and bump-toed shoes were dripping wet. Their hair hung in soggy tangles. Mascara ran down their faces.

Brianna was screaming helplessly. "My best shirt! My best skirt! My best hair!"

"I'm, like, totally soaked!" Victoria moaned.

"It's the bomb!" Mason cackled as another water balloon splattered in front of Victoria.

Suddenly, the air was filled with water balloons. Megan, Rachel, Bethany, and Natalie were the new targets.

"Ha-ha-ha-ha-ha!" laughed Mason, Tyler, and Zach.

Shrieking and yelling, the girls ran around the yard, dodging water balloons. The balloons splattered near the food tables and the volleyball net. They splattered by the garden and on the grill.

Natalie stopped.

"Revenge!" she cried, running for the hose. "*War!*" The girls flocked behind her.

Natalie brandished the hose. "Girls against boys! To the wet, sloppy end!"

"Hooray!" the girls shouted. "War on boys!"

Natalie aimed the hose at Mason, then doused Tyler and Zach.

"Let's get them!" Bethany cried, emptying a soda bottle on Jonathan's head.

"Stop! Stop! Stop!" Abby screamed, but no one listened.

Her party was racing out of control. She looked around for her parents — or even Eva and Isabel — but they had all gone inside. Alex was the only Hayes in sight.

Chapter 14

Saturday

"When the going gets rough,
remember to keep calm."

—Horace

Choppy Water Calendar

Oh, yeah? I'd like to see <u>anyone</u> keep calm when purple water balloons are flying through the air and the garden hose is turned full force on the boys!

I didn't keep calm. I was screaming like everyone else. My parents didn't hear us. Was it because we had the CD player on full blast?

No one else heard me, either.

Abby watched helplessly as Tyler got Bethany with a

water balloon and Bethany squirted him with the hose. Jessica had filled a watering can and was sprinkling Mason.

Everything was getting soaked: kids, tables, food — potato chips and popcorn, a few hot dog rolls, and the last pieces of the "Hooray! It's Summer!" cakes.

Fifth-graders were running all over the yard. Flowers were trampled. The ground was muddy. The crepe paper decorations stained the tablecloths with purple dye.

"This has to stop!" Abby cried.

If her parents saw this, they'd forbid her to ever have another party.

It was only a matter of time before they came outside again and saw the battlefield.

What could she do? Was there a bullhorn somewhere on the porch? Or an electric switch that would turn off the fighting? Or —

Abby ran down the porch steps and around to the side of the house. She found the water spigot and turned off the water. Then she unscrewed the hose.

"Hey! What happened? There isn't any more water!" Loud, disappointed cries came from the girls.

"Awwwwwwww!" The boys yelled. The last water balloons were gone.

A crowd of drenched, dripping fifth-graders stood in the Hayes backyard.

The boys looked at the girls. The girls looked at the boys.

"Now what?" Bethany asked.

There was nothing left to eat. The food was waterlogged.

There was nothing left to do. The games were wet.

There was nothing left to say.

The mood of the party was dreary and dim.

Was this how it was going to end?

Abby stood on the porch steps and surveyed the ruins of her party.

What now?

She clapped her hands for attention. The fifth-graders turned toward her.

"Announcing — "Abby began. She stopped. What was she announcing, anyway?

"For the final thirty-five minutes of the party" — she checked her watch — "for the final thirty-*seven* minutes of the party — "

"Get to the point!" Zach yelled.

"We will, um, we will — "

"Dry off?" Casey suggested.

The fifth-graders began to laugh.

"We will — " Abby began again. She had to think of *something*.

"Like, change our clothes?" Victoria suggested nastily.

"I don't have a changing room." Abby began. Her eyes lit up. "I just have a changed room!"

She took a deep breath.

"You are all invited on a tour of Abby's room!" she announced. "You are invited to see Abby's Spectacular Palace of Purple."

"Palace of Purple?" Natalie said. "I thought your room was white. With lots of calendars."

"Yes, there are lots of calendars," Abby agreed. "But in the last few weeks, I have painted the entire room — walls, furniture, and lamps — a rich, glorious purple."

Jessica's mouth dropped open.

"You did?" Natalie said. "And you didn't tell us!"

"Her room is awesome!" Alex cried.

Now she had her classmates' attention.

"Come experience the purple!" she cried. "I've transformed my dull, dingy room into a purple poem!"

* * *

The fifth-graders were lined up in the hallway outside Abby's bedroom. The line extended down the stairs and through the living room.

"Step right up! Come right in! Don't push or shove!" Abby called. "No admission charged for the Tour de Room!"

"One at a time," Casey said. He stood at the door next to Abby, making sure that kids didn't crowd in.

"This is *so* cool," Bethany said, gazing at the shiny purple.

"It's actually hot," Abby said. "I matched it to Isabel's hot purple fingernail polish."

"You did it yourself?" Zach asked admiringly. "Your parents didn't help you?"

"I did it *all*," Abby said proudly.

"It's like living inside a purple-tronic machine," Tyler said.

"What's that?" Abby asked. "I want one."

"A machine that manufactures the color purple." Tyler shrugged. "I just made it up."

Jonathan stepped inside the room. "Wow!" he yelled. "Purple power!"

Abby smiled.

"Purple Peter Piper picked a purple peck of pickled

purple peppers," Casey said to Jonathan. "Can you say that five times in a row?"

"No," Jonathan said.

"Purple Peter Piper picked a purple peck of pickled purple peppers," Casey repeated. "Purple to the max!"

"I can't believe your parents let you do this," Natalie said. "Mine would never let me."

"They weren't too happy about it," Abby confessed. "But it was too late!"

Brianna and Victoria entered the room.

"Welcome to the Palace of Purple," Abby said.

"*My* room is painted peach, with plaster molding and silk-striped wallpaper," Brianna bragged. "My mother hired an interior decorator. I have a Belgian lace canopy bed. It looks like a *real* princess room."

"Do you call this Putrid Purple?" Victoria snickered. "Or Purple Pimple?"

Mason made a rude noise. "I like it," he said. "It's loud. It's bright. It's — "

"Purple?" Zach finished for him.

Victoria's lip curled. "It's — "

"*Perfect*," Bethany finished for her.

"Was I, like, talking to you?" Victoria asked.

"Probably not," Bethany said. "Who cares?"

Victoria opened her mouth and shut it again.

"Congratulations, Abby," Brianna said. "On your party and the purple room. Victoria and I think it's *très belle*." She checked her watch. "I think my mother will be picking us up soon."

"Dingdong," Natalie said as the two of them swept out of the room.

"Good riddance to bad rubbish," Bethany muttered.

Her friends stared at her.

"Are you *serious*?" Natalie said.

Bethany nodded.

"Hooray!" Abby and Natalie said in unison.

"Do you think I should invite Ms. Bunder to see my room?" Abby asked. "Her assignment made me decide to paint."

"Sure," Jessica said. "Why not?"

"Maybe it'll give her an idea for another creative writing assignment!" Abby exclaimed. "She gets ideas from unexpected places!"

"I bet she'll love it," Bethany said.

Rachel peered into the room. "Let me guess," she said. "Your favorite color is — "

Chapter 15

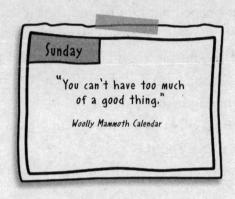

Sunday

"You can't have too much
of a good thing."

Woolly Mammoth Calendar

True or False?

1. You can't have too much purple!

2. You can't have too many kids at a party!

3. You can't have too much cake!

4. You can't have too many water balloons!

5. You can't have too many friends tour your room!

6. You can't have too much of Brianna and Victoria.

Answers:

1. True
2. True
3. True
4. False
5. True
6. False (If you got this one wrong, you are either Brianna or Victoria.)

The party is over!

Boo-hoo! How did it happen so fast?

Tomorrow, which became today, is now yesterday.

(If you can figure out what that means, you win a piece of leftover party cake! It only got a <u>little</u> wet.)

The cleanup is done.

I threw out all the paper plates and cups. I also threw out the soggy hot dog buns and the soaked decorations. I recycled the soda bottles and the plastic silverware. I put the tablecloths in the washing machine. I

dried off the games. I
reconnected the hose. I mopped
the kitchen floor where my friends
had tracked in mud. I picked up
billions of broken balloon pieces from
the yard.

Party Facts:
Watermelons eaten: 3½
Water balloons thrown: 34
Tiffany Crystal CDs played: 0 (ha-ha-ha-ha)

Hayes Book of World Records broken: 5
1. Abby wins an award for "Fastest
Thinking During Fierce Fighting."
2. Mason wins for "Sneakiest Balloon
Bombing."
3. Victoria and Brianna win for "Soggiest
Outfits."
4. Bethany wins for "Bravest Comeback."
5. My family wins the "Highest Hayes
Helper" Award! They are the best!
(They even helped me with the cleanup.)

The Hayes Family Discusses Abby's Party:

Olivia Hayes: Looks like your first party was a huge success, Abby.

Eva: Beginner's luck! You didn't have a single disaster, did you?

Abby: Uh . . .

Isabel: They liked the purple pencil party favors, didn't they?

Abby: I handed them out in my purple room.

Olivia Hayes: They'll remember the party when they write with the pencils.

Isabel: Or when they see anything purple.

Abby: I hope so!

Alex: The water balloon fight was the best!

Paul Hayes: What water balloon fight?

Abby: Uh . . .

Eva: So when are you planning the next party, Abby?

Abby: In five years?

French Dictionary (otherwise known as my older sister Isabel Hayes):

Eh bien, c'est vrai, n'est-ce pas? Well,

that's true, isn't it?

Tant pis (the "s" is silent!): Too bad

Très belle: very beautiful

(Did Brianna really say that about my room? No wonder she said it in French! She didn't want anyone to know! Maybe she liked my Purple Palace better than her designer bedroom. I bet she did!!!!!!!)

I love my purple room! I love it so much!!!! So do a lot of kids. I can't wait to invite everyone over again. I will expand my circle of friends. We will all enjoy the Purple Palace together!

Not all at once! The Hayes family won't see long lines waiting on the stairs for a peek at the purple. I will invite ONLY two or three friends at a time!